S0-AEV-745

DRIFT

TURBOC

CHARGED

DRIFT

NISSAN SKYLINE

Patrick Jones

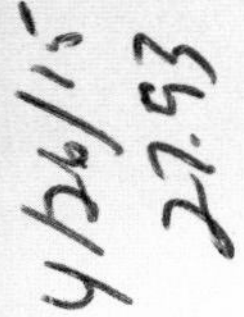

MINNEAPOLIS

Darby Creek
A division of Lerner Publishing Group, Inc.
241 First Avenue North
Minneapolis, MN 55401 U.S.A.

Website address: www.lernerbooks.com

The images in this book are used with the permisison of:
Cover and interior photograph © Maxmitzu/Dreamstime.com.

Main body text set in Janson Text LT Std 12/17.
Typeface provided by Linotype AG.

Library of Congress Cataloging-in-Publication Data

Jones, Patrick, 1961–
Drift : Nissan Skyline / by Patrick Jones.
pages cm. — (Turbocharged)
Summary: "New kid comes to town. Things get off to a rough start with the local teenage tuners. His only shot at acceptance is beating the local top dog (who buys his cars rather than builds them) at a drifting showdown on a legendary local road" — Provided by publisher.
ISBN 978-1-4677-1242-2 (lib. bdg. : alk. paper)
ISBN 978-1-4677-1667-3 (eBook)
[1. Drifting (Motorsport)—Fiction. 2. Muscle cars—Fiction. 3. Automobile racing—Fiction. 4. Racially mixed people—Fiction.]
I. Title.
PZ7.J7242Dr 2013
[Fic]—dc23 2013000977

Manufactured in the United States of America
1 – BP – 7/15/13

THANKS TO BARRY O.
AND WILLARD R. FOR
A GREAT RACE

CHAPTER ONE

Kekoa Pahinui tried not to cry as his mom passed through security at Hilo International Airport. She was on her way to the mainland to live with some guy named Ted she met online. Kekoa would live with his biodad's mom, his *kupuna wahine*, in Honolulu. He was moving from the big island to the big city.

Kekoa had been an outcast in Hilo as a half-black, half-Hawaiian kid. He couldn't imagine how he would've been treated in Ted's snow-white home of Bath, Maine. Instead, Kekoa was going to stay in Hawaii and finish his senior year. He and his mom would figure out the rest in June.

"You okay?" someone asked as Kekoa walked toward the airport parking lot.

"I'm fine," Kekoa mumbled, head down.

That's how he lived his life: head down. It hadn't helped him at his old school. Maybe because of his funny name or his biracial background, he was a bully magnet. Although he could've turned himself into an athlete or a popular kid if he had tried hard enough, some older friends from his block had shown Kekoa something far superior to sports or school success: drifting.

As he drove his light blue Nissan Skyline 350 toward the booth, Kekoa couldn't help but notice the empty parking lot on the airport's east end. He wasn't that good in math, but this was an equation he understood: his Nissan plus open pavement equaled a drifting opportunity.

Making sure no cops were around, Kekoa accelerated quickly toward the corner of the lot, where he'd need to make a sharp left turn.

Before he reached the turn, Kekoa dropped to second gear while revving the engine close to 4,000 RPMs. When Kekoa released the clutch, the surge in power made the back wheels spin so fast they lost traction with the pavement. The car's back end swung into the turn. But rather than spinning widely, Kekoa held the drift through smart steering and speed control.

Only in drifting did Kekoa experience an adrenaline surge, a sense of achievement. Before falling asleep at night, he'd fantasize about becoming a drift champion in Japan.

He earned a dirty look from the woman at the booth. That didn't surprise him. His mom didn't like drifting either. He'd done it for fun because none of his friends had any money. Like Kekoa, they lived in near poverty. Unlike people who drifted in Japan or on the islands, Kekoa couldn't tune his car's body, suspension, or even tires with new gear. He could only tune up its engine with his hands and hard work. In his wallet, he kept an article he'd printed off a school computer about ten steps to creating a drift car. He didn't know why he held on to it, since most steps took cash, but he'd memorized every word:

1. Strip the car
2. Tighten the suspension by installing stiffer springs and struts
3. Add anti-roll bars
4. Buy performance tires and wheels
5. Adjust the camber
6. Increase the engine power
7. Add cold air intake
8. Add cat-back kit
9. Add a turbocharger
10. Modify engine to improve horsepower and torque

After leaving the airport, Kekoa drove the few miles to the apartment building he'd been sharing with his mom. They'd lived in the cramped space since they lost the house. As he left his car, his glasses steamed in the August heat. He wiped them on his long white T and headed up the stairs. The warped wooden steps creaked, but not loud enough to drown out the booming rap music and the nearby roar of jets. He knew that his grandma had a nicer space for him, but better yet, she had a garage for the Nissan.

He entered the apartment and went straight to the window. It faced east, not just toward the mainland but toward his drifting paradise: the closed Lanakila Homes housing project. The homes where his childhood friends had lived were vacant, and the streets were empty. Kekoa was tempted to take one last spin, but he had to finish packing, then get to the boat that would take him and his car to Oahu.

He laughed as he thought about his drift-car list: first, strip the car. Get rid of excess weight. A good rule. He dropped two full trash bags into his car and drove off.

CHAPTER TWO

Billy Cain couldn't stop laughing as Tucker and Ryan held Keiichi Yamada's head still. "Let's cut his hair," Billy said. He nodded at Shane, who left his post at the bathroom door and handed Billy scissors. With one snip, Keiichi's pink ponytail fell from his head to the floor.

Billy pointed the scissors at Keiichi's crotch. "If you tell, it won't be your hair next time. Understand?"

When Keiichi didn't answer, Tucker and Ryan forced him to nod.

Shane moved from the door and allowed Keiichi to exit, which also allowed Mr. Steel, headmaster of White Sands Prep, to enter.

"What's going on here?" Mr. Steel asked. Everybody went silent. All eyes were on Billy. "Why is there a clump of hair on the floor?"

"Must be from one of my horses," Billy said. Mr. Steel looked at Billy like he didn't believe him. Billy flashed his student body president smile brighter.

Mr. Steel stared not at Billy but at the floor. He picked up the hair. "Get rid of it."

"Anything you say," Billy said as he picked up the ponytail. As Mr. Steel left the bathroom, Billy added, "I'll hang it on my rearview."

His pals laughed. "What happens if he tells your dad about this?" Shane asked.

Billy waved his hand, heavy with a gold senior class ring. "Steel won't talk. He knows my dad's one of the school's leading donors."

His friends fell in line behind Billy as they headed outside to wait for their rides home. The parking lot looked like a gathering of

VIPs and CEOs. Black limos and Beemers lined the winding, mile-long driveway of White Sands Prep.

* * *

"You did what?" Adam Cain bellowed at his son across the dinner table. It was a rare sight. Normally Billy's father traveled to oversee his various businesses, mostly to China, where he was opening new enterprises almost every month. "You cut a student's hair?"

"That's not true," Billy said. He wiped the sweat from his brow with the linen napkin.

"Keiichi Yamada's father called one of my people directly," Billy's father said. The words came out slowly—Adam Cain was, as always, distracted by his iPhone.

"It's not true." Billy looked at his mom. She said nothing.

"When I close a deal, I don't expect it to be broken. You stay clear at school, and I look the other way on your hobby. I can't pay off school officials *and* the police. So which is it?"

Billy bit his tongue so he wouldn't laugh. His family had enough money to pay off the school, the police, probably the entire city. But his dad seemed serious. "Okay."

"Okay, what?"

"I'll keep it together at school, and you'll look the other way on my drifting," Billy said.

"Deal done."

"Also, I need to take the Toyota in again. It's carrying too much weight, and I need new tires."

Billy's dad shook his head. "I don't understand you. You have just about everything—"

Billy tuned his dad out and looked out the big windows of their mansion in the exclusive Hawai'i Kai community. He didn't want *just about* everything. He wanted it all.

CHAPTER THREE

"*Hu'ihu'i!*" Kekoa shouted in joy as he steered his Nissan along Tantalus Mountain. Awesome. The mountain's winding roads, with stone walls on one side and a steel guardrail on the other, were famous to drifters all over Hawaii. Driveways lined the mountain at irregular intervals, with houses growing bigger and nicer closer to the top. He'd seen hundreds of videos of cars like his performing amazing drifts on crazy hairpin turns. Since this was the first time, Kekoa took it slow, just to get the feel of the road.

Drifting was about talent and timing more than speed.

He was drenched with sweat when he arrived at his grandma's place in the Kalihi neighborhood. It had been years since he'd been there, not since his grandfather's funeral four years earlier. He could tell that things had gone from bad to worse. Large industrial streets lined the way to his grandmother's house. Streets almost sure to be empty in the evening. A drifter's dream.

Kekoa took a deep breath as he parked his ride in the pitted driveway. Across the street stood a vacant house with overgrown grass and a knocked-down *For Sale* sign. On one side of it stood another house for sale, boards over the windows. On the other side was a house with broken steps, children's toys littering the front yard, and a Rottweiler chained at the neck on the porch.

It hadn't always been like this. Kekoa's grandparents had owned a nicer house in a nicer part of the city until Cain Low-Cost Auto Super Store invaded the island and crushed their small auto parts store. Rather than closing or selling out to Cain, his grandpa hung on until there was no money left in the business. Out of work, out of options, the man took his own life.

Kekoa's grandma lived simply. Kekoa was grateful she'd taken him in so he could stay in Hawaii. But as he knocked on the door, his stomach knotted up.

"Grandma!" Kekoa shouted when she greeted him. His grandma threw her skinny, heavily tanned left arm around his neck and held him tight. A lit cigarette dangled from her mouth.

"Kekoa, you look so different," she said.

Kekoa shrugged. He knew he looked pretty much the same. Only a little taller, and with a small scruff of a beard to help him look *hu'ihu'i.*

"Can I help you bring in your things?" she asked.

Kekoa broke the hug, went back to his car, and grabbed the two trash bags. "This is it."

His grandma looked puzzled. "Let me

show you to your room. It's not that big, but—"

"Actually, Grandma, I'd like to see the garage. I don't own much because everything I've ever earned went into my car. I'd feel safer if—"

"I'd hoped to hire someone to clean it out, but . . ." She sounded ashamed. "I haven't been in there since your grandfather . . . died."

Kekoa knew why: the garage was where he had left her. "I'd be happy to do it."

"That man never threw anything away," she said. "Before he lost the store, he took home as much inventory as he could. He said he would sell it, but then he couldn't let any of the parts go."

Kekoa nodded like he understood, but he didn't. He'd never had much, so he had nothing to hoard.

"Let me see how bad it is," Kekoa said.

He tried to open the door, but it was stuck. He kicked it hard, and it finally gave, but no light came on, and if there were windows, they were covered. He reached around the door, his hand knocking down spiderwebs until he found the light switch. He clicked it on and sucked in his breath. The garage was packed from floor to roof with boxes of auto parts, mostly imports.

Kekoa rubbed his eyes making sure it wasn't a mirage. It wasn't. It was a gold mine.

CHAPTER FOUR

"Awesome, brah!" Billy shouted into his phone. He tossed his book bag onto the floor of his house's foyer with such force that a vase crashed onto the tile. Still listening to Shane on the phone, he waved for Lei, one of the maids, to clean up his mess.

"DJ and dancers. Awesome!"

Billy walked the long distance from the front door to the main kitchen. He motioned to the cook to make him something to eat.

"What would you like, William?" the tiny cook asked, almost in a whisper.

"What did you say?"

"What would you like, *sir*?"

"You're the cook, you figure it out. Isn't that what I pay you for?" Billy headed over to a cabinet and pulled out four energy drinks. He stuffed two in each pocket, still talking to Shane.

"Bring it to me in the theater!" Billy shouted at the cook. He listened as Shane outlined the evening's entertainment. For Billy, the lot action was sizzle. Tantalus was the steak.

"So, normal time and place?" Shane asked.

"Right and right. Later, brah."

A huge movie screen filled the south wall of the twenty-seat theater in the east wing. Windows showing some of the best views of the island dominated the east and the west. Billy opened an energy drink with one hand. With the other, he pressed a button to close the blinds.

Before he opened the second drink, he grabbed another remote, dimmed the lights, and started *The Fast and the Furious: Tokyo*

Drift. This wasn't a movie; this would be his life. Next fall, he'd go to Harvard, like his dad had, but this summer, Billy would travel to Japan.

* * *

"I can't believe your dad supports this," Tucker said. Tucker was new to Billy's clique.

Billy didn't like Tucker, but he had designs on Tucker's maid's daughter, a pudgy but pretty Kenyan girl named Adila. Billy, Shane, and Ryan had a thousand-dollar bet on who could hook up with her first.

"I get this if I don't get in trouble at school." Billy started to laugh. "Well, bad trouble."

"And the police?" Tucker shouted over the music. The DJ who Shane had hired pounded out beats through the parking garage of the White Circle Mall, owned by Cain Inc.

Billy explained how his dad let him, his friends, and select others use the garage. Billy told his dad they didn't race; they just showed off their cars. His dad kept the cops away with cash.

"He said he would build a real racetrack, but he didn't," Billy said. "My dad lies."

"You ready, champ?" Shane asked. He tossed Billy his racing helmet. Billy hated wearing the helmet, but he did just in case.

"Go easy on me," Shane said. "I need a new anti-roll bar, but they're hard to find."

Billy grunted. He never went easy on anyone. Fifty kids from White Sands Prep moved to the side as Shane and Billy started their cars. Shane drove an orange Toyota Supra. Billy climbed into a bright red Toyota Altezza, the best drift car in the world.

With a roaring of engines and a cloud of exhaust, Shane and Billy started racing through the three-story garage. At the first corner, Billy tapped the brake with his right foot, which transferred the vehicle weight to the front wheels for traction. He turned the wheel right. With his left foot, Billy pressed down the clutch and then pulled the emergency brake for a second, which locked up the rear wheels. While the car slid, Billy turned the wheel hard to the left and then punched the accelerator pedal. He knew everyone watching was in awe of him, which made perfect sense. Billy knew he was perfectly awesome.

CHAPTER FIVE

"You drift?" a skinny haole kid asked Kekoa in the school parking lot.

As Kekoa unlocked the door to his Nissan, he wished he could reverse his decision to drive the car to school. The first thing he had installed was a new anti-theft system, but as Kekoa knew from his friends back in Hilo, if you wanted a car bad enough, you could always steal it.

"Just curious, my bad." The kid flashed the all-purpose *shaka* sign. "*Da kine*, brah."

"What's your name?" Kekoa asked.

Normally he didn't like white kids who adopted Hawaiian signs and words, but something about the guy seemed real.

The kid extended his hand. "Sonny." Kekoa noted the dirt under his nails, maybe grease. He shook the kid's hand. Sonny was strong. So was the stink from his clothes.

"I just asked 'cause I see you got the 350. That's one of the best drift cars. Maybe not *the* best. I'd say that the best cars are all Toyotas, starting with the Altezza, then the Corolla, then—"

Kekoa put up his hand like a stop sign. "So, which do you drive?"

Sonny pulled out his pockets. "No cash means no car."

"I know how you feel," Kekoa said out of habit. The truth was he had money on the way. He'd made a deal with his grandma. They'd sell the parts in the garage on Craigslist and split the proceeds. Grandma entered the parts into the computer, and Kekoa met the customer after school. Kekoa guessed anyone with enough money to buy parts to mod their car wouldn't venture into Kalihi at night.

"I'd like to build a car from scratch, but that's hard to do, especially without a base," Sonny said.

"I see videos of people drifting here," Kekoa asked. "You know any of them?"

"There's a scene by Pearl that's a mix of Japanese kids and navy brats. Then there's one I've only heard about at some mall where all these rich posers race, and then there's—"

"Tantalus Mountain."

"That's the real scene. But since I've got no car, I've just seen the vids. Looks wild."

Although Kekoa had avoided making enemies at his new school, three weeks in, he'd yet to meet a friend. "You asked me if I drifted, right? Well, if you want to find out, how about we hit Tantalus tonight?"

"Icy!" Sonny said. They exchanged digits and talked until the sun set over the Pacific.

"There's somebody at the door about a part," Kekoa's grandma shouted into the garage.

Kekoa looked at his phone. It was almost ten at night. He wiped the grease from his hands and started toward the door. He'd hoped his grandma would be asleep by now so he could sneak out.

"Send them around back!" Kekoa said as he walked through the maze of boxes toward the side door. He'd moved some stuff into the attic to make room for his ride.

He peeked through the dirty window before he opened the door. While all the parts he was selling were from his grandfather's old store, that didn't mean the cops wouldn't hassle him.

"Who is it?"

The figure outside was chubby and wore a San Fran Giants ball cap down low. Skin that looked dark like Kona coffee. Lots of bracelets but no tats. Probably not a banger.

"I need a part," the voice said. High pitched, really young. Kekoa opened the door.

The girl passed him a note with her blistered hands.

Kekoa opened the note. "*Anti-roll bar for 1987 Toyota Supra.* Is this for you?"

The girl turned her hat around. She was pretty, with a nice smile, thick eyebrows, and big brown eyes behind small glasses with silver rims. "I don't think so," she laughed.

"I don't do business with people I don't know. What's your name?" Kekoa asked.

"Adila," she answered. Kekoa smiled. Sonny had made his day, but Adila owned the night.

CHAPTER SIX

"I'm ready to go now," Shane said.

"Where'd you get the part?" Billy asked.

"Some *hapa* in the hood. Tucker paid Adila to do it. No way I'd go."

Billy laughed at Shane. "Mistake, man. You could've showed off for Adila. Yet another reason I'll win that bet."

"We'll see what you have tonight," Shane said, but Billy cut him down with a glare.

Just like the week before, Billy and his friends gathered at the mall. Once again, Shane had hired a DJ. But unlike the previous

Saturday, when Billy's dad was in town and Billy needed to get home at a decent hour, there were no rules. He was the man of the mall lot, but he longed to be king of the mountain.

"If you need anything for your cars, let Tucker know. Or I could help," Shane said.

"I'll have Adila take me. Then I'll take her to paradise," Billy said.

Shane laughed. "You're the man, Billy, that's for sure."

After the hangers-on and spectators left the mall, no doubt impressed with Billy's abilities, it was time for the real fun of the night. They rode to Tantalus. Billy led the way. On the drive up, he talked nonstop to Tucker, who was three cars behind, as Billy tried to figure out the best way forward with Adila. Nothing he'd tried so far had worked, which he couldn't stand. Billy didn't lose at anything. It wasn't a matter of if he'd get what he wanted but when.

"Okay, Tucker, you set it up, but you better concentrate now, son," Billy said, then hung up as they reached the base of the mountain. No time for talk. Time for action. Time to drift.

The winding mountain road—recently resurfaced, thanks to Billy's father's friends on the city council—had been featured in several video games. As his Toyota sped up the mountain, Billy thought about all the people beneath him who would never know the rush of drifting except through video games or YouTube. He turned on the camera in his car just before the first big turn. Big not only for the angle but for the risk.

Billy had learned to drift through trial and error on the grounds of his estate and the school driveway, striking the right balance. A few cars and few years later, he was becoming the maestro of the mountain.

He hit the first turn perfectly, yanking the emergency brake and then steering into the drift. He maintained control even as the steering wheel spun like an out-of-control roulette wheel at one of his dad's Hong Kong casinos. Behind him, Billy heard the squeal of tires and breathed the smell of rubber.

Each turn he added more speed, knowing his ride was perfectly balanced. The best mechanics on the island had turned his Toyota into a drifting machine. As his car skidded from side to side, Billy thought about those losers racing in the streets in a straight line for ten seconds or going around in circles for hours. Drifting was about side-to-side motion. Like a turbocharged game of squash where the driver was the ball, bouncing back and forth.

At the top of the mountain, Billy pulled onto the small shoulder of the road. He climbed out of the car and sucked in the night air, but it did nothing to get the smell of burnt rubber out of his nose. Just like his anti-roll bar stabilized his ride, drifting this mountain stabilized his life. And the top spot provided his favorite view: looking down on everyone else.

CHAPTER SEVEN

"Drifting is a sport for losers," Sonny laughed.
Kekoa rolled his eyes. "What are you talking about?" he asked as he handed Sonny the wrench. They were putting in a passenger's seat so Sonny could ride along when Kekoa drifted on Tantalus Mountain.

"Your car is a one-seater, so it's a great car for a loser without friends or a girlfriend."

Kekoa broke the stare and laughed along, in part because he realized Sonny was right. But even though he didn't have any new friends except Sonny and no girlfriend—until he got up the courage to call Adila—he didn't feel like a loser. "So, let's hit that mall you told me about. The action pretty good?"

Sonny set down the wrench and pulled out his phone. He loaded a video of cars drifting at White Circle Mall. He and Kekoa studied each drift carefully.

"Look at the red Altezza go!" Kekoa said.

"That guy's using the e-brake," Sonny explained. "Real drifters, the best ones, consider that almost cheating, but then, these guys don't compete."

"Well, that's something I guess we have in common," Kekoa said. "Unless you go to Japan and race professionally, we're just showing off. Even that mall stuff isn't a real race."

"Trust me, I know something about these guys. We have nothing in common with them."

Kekoa grunted as he tightened the bolt on the seat belt holder. "They drift, so do I, and you will too one day. They use a vacant garage, but we'll use empty project streets."

Sonny put the phone back in his pocket and started back to work on the seat. "The mall's not vacant."

"Then how are they—"

"I heard one of the kids' dad owns it. He lets him and his pals use it."

"Must be nice to have that."

"Money?" Sonny asked.

"No, a dad who does things for you."

After testing out a new stabilizer they'd installed, Kekoa and Sonny made their way to the vacant project roads. Kekoa had never drifted with someone in the car with him, so he was tentative, almost afraid. But Sonny was having the time of his life.

"Man, this is great," Sonny shouted as he breathed in the fumes. "It's like being a pair of Chucks inside a clothes dryer, and the rubber souls are burning. This is sweet."

"If I'm going to show this baby off, I'm gonna need some performance tires."

"I know the best place," Sonny said. "And they're even legal!"

"Unlike this!" Kekoa shouted as he pressed on the accelerator, heading for the turn. Kekoa steered the car to the outside of the turn on the approach. This moved the weight to the outside wheels. Sensing the wheels losing traction, Kekoa quickly steered into the turn. When the car's suspension kicked back, the weight shifted so quickly that the back end flicked out to start the drift. "It's a feint drift but ain't nothing fake about it!"

"You're good at this," Sonny said. He was almost hyperventilating.

"And I want to get better," Kekoa said.

"Only one way to do that: you gotta get pushed. Pedal to the metal."

"As you wish!"

The next section of road was long, the perfect place to get up speed for a Kansei drift. He entered the turn at 70 MPH, then released the gas pedal. He felt the jolt as the car's weight shifted to its front wheels, initiating a drift as the rear tires lost traction. Sonny looked scared, but not Kekoa. He was in control even of an out-of-control car.

CHAPTER EIGHT

"These are the best, the very best, right?" Billy asked the salesman at RAD Motorsports.

"For performance tires for your vehicle, absolutely," the timid salesman said.

"They have to function and look good. I'm all about looking good."

Shane, Tucker, and Ryan laughed. All four were dressed in white shorts and red polo shirts from their country club. "And rims—I want some sweet chrome, not that gaudy crap you sold me last time."

"As I told you, Mr. Cain, I'll provide you

with a store credit," the salesman said as he pasted on a typical salesman smile.

"Okay, I'll get 'em on the Altezza today and bring in my other cars later, understand?"

The salesman nodded. Billy grabbed his wallet and pulled out the Platinum AmEx card.

"Don't worry about that, Mr. Cain. It's all taken care of. Thank you for your business."

Billy shrugged. He led the way outside, where his Altezza was parked. He pulled it slowly into the garage and then tossed the keys to the mechanic. "Don't F it up."

The mechanic lowered his eyes. Billy joined his friends in the parking lot. Tucker sat in the driver's seat of his gold Lexus, his non-drift car, while Ryan and Shane sat in the back. When Billy got in the passenger's seat, Shane handed him an energy drink.

"Where to?" Tucker asked.

"Wherever we want, I guess," Billy said. Everybody laughed. "Your place, Tucker. Just in case Adila might stop by. You think you could arrange that?"

Tucker paused. “I don’t know, my mom might not like—”

“Man up, Tucker,” Billy said.

“Right, man up,” Shane and Ryan said at the same time.

“If you want to hang with us, you’d better learn to be a little more cooperative,” Billy said. He had the tone of a parent speaking to a young child.

Tucker dropped his head down. “Sorry, Billy. Sure, I’ll figure something out.”

“Maybe you could bring her with you next Saturday,” Billy suggested.

“But my Silvia only has one seat.”

“Strap her to the top!” Shane said.

“Or maybe you bring her in the Lexus and just watch. If you do that, then maybe next time we do the mountain, I’ll let you follow behind me. How does that sound?” Billy asked.

“Whatever you say,” Tucker said.

Billy gulped down the energy drink, rolled down the window, and tossed out the empty can. Before it hit the pavement, Shane handed him another one.

"Hey, Billy, is that guy going to make you pay for those tires or what?" Shane asked.

Billy popped the can's tab. "He's one of the few independent auto stores in town, so."

"So, why doesn't your dad just buy him out?" Ryan asked.

Billy laughed. "Ryan, don't you know anything? If you put him out of business, then what do you have? Nothing. But if he's in business, I let him know he's vulnerable, then what?"

The car went silent except for the ever-present hip-hop booming bass.

"He's like Adila's mom," Billy said. "He's powerless, but he thinks he's free. As long as people think that way, then the better for all of us." The car exploded in laughter.

"Good one, Billy," Tucker said.

Billy poked his finger in Tucker's shoulder. "Not just good. The best."

CHAPTER NINE

"Did you feel the difference?" Sonny asked as Kekoa finished up a jump drift.

"Where were you when I needed you back in Hilo?"

Kekoa felt ready to leave the project streets and make his way out toward Pearl Harbor Naval Base. While there was still more work to be done on the car, which required both money and time, Kekoa wanted to introduce himself to the drifting scene sooner rather than later. Also maybe drum up some auto part business.

"In my house, reading about drifting when I should've been doing homework," Sonny said. "You got to be rich or connected, and I'm neither."

"But you're smart," Kekoa said.

"About cars, yeah. Everything else, not so much."

"Explain again why this drifts so much better?" Kekoa asked. He drove out toward Pearl carefully. In Hilo, his friends were always getting pulled over for speeding and then getting tickets for making illegal modifications. Kekoa drove the limit and stayed free of the cops.

"Camber angle, the angle of wheel, impacts how the wheel contacts the road," Sonny started. Kekoa listened as Sonny explained how the aggressive negative camber setting in the front wheels improved tracking during counter-steering and improved turn-in capacity. A negative camber setting burned up tires quicker, added risk, and made drifting better. "I guess since you have negative settings in the back and the front, two wrongs to make a right."

Kekoa looked quickly to see there were no police around as he and Sonny drove down the large industrial streets on the way to Pearl.

"I better enjoy this now 'cause we'll need to get this seat out of here at Pearl," Sonny said.

"I'm up for that!" Kekoa said, then launched into another drift on the open road.

* * *

Kekoa lowered the music as he pulled into the big open lot not far from Pearl Harbor. Just as Sonny had described, it was a mix of Asian kids, probably Japanese, and white guys with short hair.

Sonny pointed toward the entrance. "It looks like they're fighting World War II again."

"Yeah, except Japan won. Everybody's driving their cars," Sonny laughed.

"What was this place?" Kekoa stared at the huge vacant lot.

"I don't know," Sonny answered. "I heard it was going be used for solar power, but some of the bigwigs in town make too much money importing oil, so that ain't happening."

A big crowd had gathered around a makeshift drift-racing track. Guys raced two at a time, producing clouds of exhaust and smoke. Kekoa parked, and then he and Sonny walked over to the crowd, trying to blend in.

"Hey, who invited you?" some guy with a crew cut shouted at Kekoa.

"We'd heard this was the place to be," Sonny answered. The guy glared at Kekoa.

"How old are you guys?" Crew Cut asked.

"Old enough," Kekoa answered, glaring back.

The guy nodded, smiled, and stepped back.

"You got judges, or just running for fun?" Kekoa asked.

"No judges, no rules, no fees. Just a bunch of guys blowing off steam. Well I guess there's one rule."

"What's that?" Sonny asked.

"Nobody just watches, because that's how you get snitches," Crew Cut said, still looking at Kekoa as if Sonny didn't exist. "You wanna watch, you gotta drift. You got a car?"

"It's not a car," Kekoa pointed at his ride. "It's a 350 and a lean, mean drifting machine."

CHAPTER TEN

"These are my friends, Billy, Shane, and Ryan," Tucker shouted over the music in the mall parking garage as he parked his Acura next to Billy's Toyota.

"And who is this?" Billy leaned in the open passenger's side window.

"Adila," Adila said. Billy motioned for Shane and Ryan to back away from the car, which they quickly did.

"What a pretty name. What does it mean?" Billy asked.

Adila looked at the floor of the car. Billy

didn't like when people didn't make eye contact with him.

"It is Swahili," Adila said. "It means 'justice.'"

Billy's ever-present smile dimmed for a moment, but he switched it back on. "Did Tucker here tell you what you get to experience tonight?"

Adila nodded. Billy leaned closer. "So why haven't we seen you down here before?"

"I'm awfully busy," Adila said.

"Let me guess, with a modeling career? Where you been, Paris? Rome?"

Adila giggled. "I'm not a model."

Billy shook his head. "Well, you should be, that's for sure. You should let me help."

Adila sighed and turned toward Tucker. "You guys are all alike."

"What are you talking about?" Billy said.

"You trust fund kids, you think everybody wants your help. I don't need it," Adila said. "I thought maybe one of you might be different, but I can tell that's not the case."

Billy put himself at eye level with Adila.

He smiled like his dad taught him—the best way he knew to close a deal. "You're right. Most of us are the same. But you can trust me."

Adila laughed and Billy's smile crashed. "Tucker, take me home, please."

"What was that?" Billy shouted at Tucker when Tucker returned an hour later, this time in his black and white Nissan Silvia S13. "You embarrassed me. You should leave."

"Hey, I said I'd bring her," Tucker say, sounding hurt. "That's all I was supposed to do."

"Good thing that Shane and Ryan didn't hear any of that," Billy said. "You don't say anything, and I'll let you stay."

"You said I could follow you up the mountain. What about that?" Tucker asked.

"I like to drift, Tucker. I don't like to be pushed," Billy said. "Know your place."

* * *

Billy raced toward the road up Tantalus. Tucker fell in behind, with Shane third, Ryan fourth. With a light rain falling, only a few of the other White Sands drifters joined the caravan. By the time Billy reached Tantalus Road, the rain was falling harder, but he wasn't worried. He had skills and courage the others lacked. He'd show Tucker.

Even in the rain, Billy nailed some tight drifts at the start. When he reached the one long straight section of the road, he decided it would be a perfect location to put Tucker in his place. The engine of Billy's Toyota roared as he hit 90 MPH. He pulled the emergency brake, sending his car into a perfect drift back and forth on the wet road. He pulled out of the drift, looked in his rearview, and waited to see Tucker's distinctive headlights. And waited. And waited.

CHAPTER ELEVEN

"This is the life," Kekoa said. He adjusted his blue headband, which was damp with sweat. He and Sonny had spent an entire Saturday working on the Skyline's engine. "If I'm going to hit some killer drifts, I've got to get this baby tuned so every plug and point is perfect."

"K, you won't be the show until you get a new turbo," Sonny said.

"I know, I know, but I don't have a kit in this garage. I'll need to buy it, and I just don't have the scratch together yet," Kekoa said. "Sales are slowing down."

"Well, when you rock it tonight, people will see," Sonny added.

"I'm gonna crush it, no doubt."

Kekoa put his head back under the hood and listened to the engine hum. It was like music.

They had modified everything small with the parts on hand: new air filter, hoses, fuel pump, fuel injector, and much more. Sonny had drawn up the list, and they'd worked piece by piece until the Skyline 350 was 350 percent improved.

Kekoa loved listening to the engine, but he wished he could listen to something else almost as beautiful: that girl who came to buy parts. He had her number, but he couldn't bring himself to call.

Sonny joined Kekoa under the hood, tightening every bolt. "Only one problem, K."

"What's that?"

"Cops might crack down after that thing last weekend," Sonny said.

Kekoa looked puzzled. "What thing?"

"K, if you're gonna drift here, you gotta

get hooked up with the scene," Sonny said. He told Kekoa about an accident on Tantalus Road the past Sunday morning. "All the reports say that folks in the neighborhood heard the sounds of people drifting just before."

"That sucks," Kekoa said. "Somebody get hurt?"

"Somebody died. Kid who went to White Sands," Sonny said. "Every time there's an accident, the cops bust things up. We might show up out by Pearl tonight and see it's empty."

When Sonny went inside to go to the bathroom, Kekoa pulled out his phone. He brought up the girl's number and took a deep breath. You drifted alone in your car, but not through life. It was time to tune his status quo.

As he listened to the dial tone, he thought again about the accident. Unlike whatever kid crashed and died, Kekoa had more skills and more sense. You don't drift in the rain on a mountain road. He knew that, so how come some White Sands kid didn't?

"Hello. Um, is this the girl who bought an anti-roll bar recently?" Kekoa asked.

There was silence on the other end. "I can't talk now. Later."

Kekoa's heart revved faster than his Nissan. "When?"

"After the funeral," the girl said in a whisper.

CHAPTER TWELVE

"Dad, I swear I don't know anything about it!" Billy shouted. His words echoed off the walls of the limousine taking them to Tucker's funeral. "We hang out at the mall, that's it."

"Then what was he doing up on that mountain road?"

"I don't know because I wasn't there. Look, Dad, why would I do that? Why would I ruin a good thing? Do you think I'm that stupid? You know I'm smart, right? I'm your son."

Billy's father nodded, smiled, and then went back to his phone.

* * *

"I can't believe he messed this up for us," Billy said to Shane and Ryan as they stood outside the Church of Prosperity, the biggest mega-church on the island. With the sun beating down on them, they began to sweat in their black suits, but none of them as much as Billy.

"What a selfish tool," Ryan offered.

Billy didn't reply. His thoughts were already elsewhere. Adila stood with her mom and other servants.

"Brah, it's steaming out here. Let's get inside," Ryan said. "Maybe the sooner we're in, the sooner we'll get out. I got stuff to do."

Billy pointed toward the church. "You guys go in. I'm waiting for someone."

"You going to say something to Tucker's dad?" Shane asked. "Tell him we're sorry. You'll take the lead, as always."

"If I see him, I sure will." Billy's eyes scanned the sea of white faces in black suits until he spotted the person he was looking for.

Not Tucker's father but Adila.

"I'm so sorry for your loss," Billy whispered to Adila's mother. "I know that many of my—I mean, you get to know someone working for—I mean, with them. So, I'm sorry."

"Thank you, young man," Adila's mother said softly.

"My name is Billy Cain. Tucker was a friend of mine." Billy kept talking so he could continue walking with Adila and her mother. When Adila arrived at the pew where most of the other servants sat, Billy followed close behind.

All through the service, Billy didn't look at the closed coffin but at Adila's closed eyes. He tried to remember their color. He wondered if she took off her glasses when she kissed. As the preacher spoke of the richness of the next life, Billy thought of his. As the service ended, Billy watched Adila's eyes produce a tear. Billy concentrated and squeezed one out himself.

When the service was over, Billy walked

outside with Adila and her mom, his arm on her mom's arm. He walked them all the way to their car, a blue-and-rust Impala. Showing his good manners, Billy opened the door for Adila's mom and then walked over to do the same for Adila.

Billy stood next to her and whispered. "After a few days, you and I should get together."

Adila took a step back. She covered her face.

Billy reached out and touched her hands. "Don't worry. I can make it okay."

Adila pulled her hands away and slapped Billy's face.

"Don't you know who I am?" Billy said. He smiled large to fight off the pain and shock.

"Yes, but more than that, I know *what* you are."

"What does that mean?"

"You're a taker. You take from people who work hard to serve you. You take away people's dignity and respect. You take and take but give nothing in return."

Billy smiled. "I guess that's why I have everything, and you'll always have nothing."

CHAPTER THIRTEEN

"Some way to spend a Saturday night," Kekoa joked.

Adila laughed, again. She'd laughed at most of the things he'd said. Kekoa knew he'd tried too hard with girls in the past. The secret to getting girls to look at you was simple: be yourself and keep the pressure off. They'd met in the morning for coffee but ended up spending the day together.

"Well, it's only the beginning," Sonny added. "They want to see you drift? Wait until they see what this car can do with the new cold air intake system."

"This is Hawaii. There's never any cold air to intake!" Adila said. She sat on a stool a few feet away. She wore a long white sleeveless dress, sandals, and her Giants ball cap.

"That's why you need a baller fender mount like we installed," Sonny said.

"How does cold air make your car better?" Adila asked.

Kekoa smiled. "It's for the engine. The colder the air, the denser it is. More density, more oxygen. More oxygen, more power. It's science!"

Adila laughed. "Well to me, it's just noise."

Kekoa closed the hood, got into the 350, and turned it on. It roared louder, meaner than before. He loved the hard steel rev of the engine, but the soft sound of Adila's laughter was just as welcome.

While Sonny finished reconnecting the intake snorkel, Kekoa and Adila sat on the porch outside.

"I'm glad you called," Adila said. "What school you go?"

"Farrington. How about you?" Kekoa asked. He tried to sit as close to her as he could. As much as Kekoa loved the smell of the drift, the drifting scent of Adila's perfume was sweeter.

"Waipahu High. We could've gone to high school together if Mom and I hadn't moved. We used to live there." Adila pointed at the closed-down projects.

"I guess somehow, some way, we were gonna meet up, don't you think?" Kekoa asked in a whisper.

"Maybe, Kekoa, maybe." Adila laughed and touched his arm. "Fate?"

"Fate is superstition. I'm a man of science and action!" Kekoa said. Adila moved closer.

Adila lifted her left eyebrow "Action?"

"Action," Kekoa whispered as he turned her ball cap backward and kissed her lips.

"So how do you work it?" Kekoa asked the crew cut guy, whose name he'd learned was Jack O'Brien. Kekoa drove over in the Skyline, while Sonny and Adila followed in Adila's Impala.

Jack explained the scene at Pearl. While people raced in tandem, there weren't judges or anything. It was all for kicks, no betting, just a chance to show off cars and skills.

"How can it be a race if you don't pick winners or losers?" Kekoa asked. If he wanted to compete in Japan, he'd need some real racing experience. This was close, but not it.

Jack laughed and punched Kekoa lightly on the arm. "Trust me, everybody knows."

"So, how about me and you?"

Jack laughed again. "Listen, kid, I'm the best there is."

Kekoa stared back at Jack. "If you think you're better than me, accept the challenge. Let's drift!"

CHAPTER FOURTEEN

Billy gulped from an energy drink and pointed to the mall parking lot's smaller-than-usual crowd. "I wonder if they're afraid of getting caught."

"Or maybe of dying," Ryan said. Billy met him with a hard stare.

"Hey, Tucker knew the risks. We all knew the risks. It's his fault, not mine," Billy said.

"What do you think about hitting Tantalus tonight?" Shane asked Billy.

Billy shook his head. "Nah. I bet that road is filled with cops. Now, are we going to drift or sit around feeling sorry for ourselves?" Billy asked.

Ryan and Shane looked at each other, but Billy knew the answer. They'd do whatever he wanted them to do.

Billy only broke off a few awesome drifts before the sound of the Toyota's revving engine was overcome by sirens screaming in the night sky. When the first cruisers hit the mall, Billy watched some of the White Sands kids roar off in the opposite direction. Even Ryan ran away. Billy and Shane were in a tandem drift, but both stopped when the cops got close.

Billy pushed his car into park and climbed out, hands up. It was just like a scene from one of the *Fast and Furious* movies. Except Billy wasn't some hood. He was a Cain.

Two officers exited their car, lights still flashing.

"This is private property!" a white

cop with the big belly shouted. "You're trespassing."

Billy laughed. "You're right. It is private property. My family owns it."

Shane left his car and stood next to Billy. "Is there a problem, officer?" Shane asked.

"You're creating a public disturbance," the second cop, part Hawaiian, said.

"Is there a fine?" Billy asked. He reached into his pocket. "Just getting my wallet."

"One hundred dollars," the white cop said. The other nodded in agreement.

Billy reached into his wallet and counted out five twenty-dollar bills. "Oh, wait there's two of us breaking the law. Well, to be honest, officer, four of us in all. So that's four hundred total."

Billy kept counting bills until he reached that amount. "I'd like to pay it now."

The two cops looked at each other, then back at Billy. The white cop reached out his hand and took the money from Billy. "You best be getting along now, understand?"

"Shane, let's say we wanted to continue this. Where might we go?" Billy asked.

Again the officers looked at each other, seeing who'd be the first to blink.

"By Pearl, where they were going to build that solar thing. Roll down a window. You'll hear it," the white cop said.

"Billy high-fived Shane again, and they returned to their cars. As Billy pulled out of the ramp, he looked at the massive tire skids left on the pavement. He was like Picasso, and those marks were his masterpieces.

Billy told Shane to call around, get more information about the Pearl location, and then round everyone up. They'd meet up again, except for Ryan, who Billy told Shane not to call. By midnight, most of the While Sands crew had reassembled at a closed gas station.

"Follow me!" Billy shouted.

As always, Shane and the others did as Billy told them.

CHAPTER FIFTEEN

"You can do all that without turbo? I'm impressed," Jack said to Kekoa.

They'd raced in tandem ten times, and Kekoa knew that even in a lesser car, he was the more skilled driver. Better than that, Kekoa could tell by the sound of Jack's voice that Jack had learned the same hard truth.

"I just need a little bit more cash, and then I'm unstoppable," Kekoa said.

Jack offered Kekoa a beer, but Kekoa waved it away. The thrill of victory had him buzzed.

"Tell me in that last turn, how did you do that?" Jack said. "I mean, that was one serious drift."

Kekoa explained the basic concepts of brake drifting, the most complex type of drifting and also the most successful. "The key is footwork. Too much, you stop before you drift and understeer. Too little, you don't worry about understeering—you worry about the undertaker!"

"Heel-toe."

"I don't dance, but that's what it's like. It's all in the footwork: right-foot toe on brake, heel on gas, and left foot on the clutch. Once you face the corner, you hit the gas and you got it."

"Man, it's the best feeling in the world!" Jack shouted.

"You're out of control but also in control. Planned chaos and random direction."

Jack saluted Kekoa with a final swig of his beer and headed back toward his car. Kekoa savored the moment, letting Jack's words bounce around in his head. Then he wiped the sweat of his forehead, then waved to Sonny and Adila to join him. They'd watched from the sidelines.

"I don't think I can watch you do this. It's too scary," Adila said.

"It's only scary if you don't know what you're doing." Kekoa said. "But I do."

"Before we come back here, we gotta get that turbocharger installed," Sonny said.

Kekoa knew they were way short of the money they needed. "A good kit is 5K, easy, and I can't sell that many parts. We need to find another way to raise the money."

"I need to go," Adila said as she tugged on Kekoa's arm.

"I'm done for the night. Ain't nobody better than me," Kekoa said, but before he could return to his car, he saw headlights in the distance. Not cops—the sound coming from the cars wasn't sirens but loud booming music. The lead car was a red Toyota. The small caravan of six cars circled the track a few times. All of them were drift cars, and all of them were far nicer on the outside than

Kekoa's ride. The navy brats and the Japanese who had been racing pulled to the side.

"I know that car," Adila said.

"Who is it?" Kekoa asked, but the car looked familiar to him too, from some YouTube videos.

"Billy Cain." Adila shuddered as if a cold wind had blown in with the cars.

"Who is he?" Kekoa asked. Sonny, standing a few feet behind the couple, laughed. Kekoa turned to face him, but Adila's eye remained focused on the lead car. No longer content to just circle, the red car started to show off, performing spectacular drifts.

"His dad owns like half the island," Sonny said. "I didn't know he did drifting."

"My mom is the cook for one of his friend's family," Adila said. Over the roar of the revving engines and squealing tires, Adila told Kekoa everything she knew about Billy Cain, except how he'd hit on her at Tucker's funeral. She told him things her mom had heard while working for Tucker's parents about Billy's antics at school. Kekoa pounded his fists together when she told a story about Billy and his friends bullying a kid named Keiichi Yamada in the bathroom.

Kekoa said nothing as the lead car grew closer, a red Toyota Altezza that looked like a million dollars. The car finally stopped in front of Kekoa, Sonny, and Adila.

CHAPTER SIXTEEN

"So what did you think?" Billy asked no one in particular as he climbed out of his car. Behind him, Shane and the others exited their cars too. They all left their engines humming.

"Nice wheels," some guy in a crew cut said. A couple other crew cut types, as well as a bunch of Asian gearheads, walked toward Billy's ride.

"Did you e-brake?" somebody shouted over the noise.

When Billy scanned the crowd to find

the source of the comment, he was stunned to see Adila. He pushed his way through the onlookers and moved toward her. She stood next to a half-black, half-Hawaiian kid and a white kid who dressed ghetto.

"What are you doing here?" Billy asked. "I didn't know you were into this scene."

"She's not. I am," the *hapa* said as he pulled Adila closer to him. Adila was taller.

"Really. And which of these hunks of metal do you drive?" Billy asked.

The *hapa* pointed toward a blue Nissan.

"I used to own one of those but then got myself a real drift car," Billy said.

"How long did it take you to tune it so it rides so fine?" the skinny white kid asked.

"Let me guess, you're one of those built-it-from-scratch types?" Billy asked.

Both of the guys nodded. Billy shook his head. "Well, if you want to do things the hard way . . ."

"You mean the right way."

This guy had a big mouth for a *hapa*, Billy thought. Some people just didn't know their place. Billy would have to teach him the hard way.

"You think your oversized model car is better than my ride?" Billy scoffed at the idea.

"One way to find out." The *hapa* walked past Billy. Adila and the white kid followed. Billy turned his back and started toward his car. As if on cue, the other White Sands racers did the same. Billy waited until Shane was by his side to explain what had taken place.

⁂ ⁂ ⁂

"You can't let him trash-talk you that way, Billy," Shane said. "You can smoke these guys. Everybody knows you're the best drifter on the island. These guys are too chicken to run our course or tackle Tantalus."

"Let's see his ride," Billy said. He motioned for Shane to follow. The two inspected the Nissan Skyline 350.

"Not bad, not bad," Billy said. "I like the fender mount. Let's see the inside."

Billy wasn't sure where Adila went, but

he would be fine with never seeing her again. Any girl that didn't want to get with him, Billy thought, was too dumb to get with in the first place. Some people just had no taste.

The skinny kid popped the hood. Billy laughed. "What no turbo? No nitrous?"

"Cost too much and doesn't really help, except for how the drift looks," the *hapa* said.

Billy laughed, then turned toward Shane, who laughed even harder. "Drifting is all about how things look. The more tricks, the more you scare the competition."

"You mean like using the e-brake all the time? To me, that's cheating," the *hapa* said.

"What, you never do an e-brake drift?" Billy said.

"I drift by knowing my ride, not by taking shortcuts. But maybe you're used to taking shortcuts," the *hapa* said, getting up in Billy's face.

"Do you know who you're talking to?" Billy said.

"Yea, I'm talking to Billy Cain."

The guy smiled. His teeth were crooked,

his hair was messy, and his clothes were dirty. A real lowlife, Billy thought.

"That's right. And who are you, big mouth?" Billy asked.

"Kekoa Pahinui." Kekoa crossed his arms over his chest. "If that's too hard to pronounce with that silver spoon in your mouth, let's compete. Then you can call me winner."

CHAPTER SEVENTEEN

"So why do you think he didn't accept my challenge?" Kekoa asked. They sat on the back porch of Kekoa's grandma's house, sipping ice tea loaded with sugar.

Adila laughed. "I don't think people like him are used to being challenged. They're so used to getting their way that everybody's afraid to talk back to them."

Kekoa shrugged his shoulders. "I'm lucky. He's probably got a lot more horses under the hood than me. Better tires, better everything."

Adila kissed Kekoa's cheek. "The whole thing scares me."

"If you have skills, nobody gets hurt."

"What about Billy's friend Tucker?" Adila whispered.

Kekoa pulled Adila tight toward him. "Those guys with him the other night, they're not his friends. They're just his toadies."

"More like his accomplices. I know Tucker was involved in that thing I told you about."

"Did that Japanese kid ever do anything? Did they get in trouble?" Kekoa asked.

"Not that I know of."

"Do you know anything else about that kid they bullied?"

Adila shook her head. "No, but I bet my mom could find out. Why?"

"Um, I gotta call Sonny," Kekoa said. "I think I'm going to be busy for a while working on my ride, but if you want to hang out with us . . ."

"What could be more fun that watching you and Sonny fix a car?"

"Most everything, I suppose."

Kekoa and Adila laughed as the night fell from the sky.

* * *

"Sweet!" Sonny said when he visited Kekoa in his garage a few days later. He stood in awe of the turbocharger kit ready for installation. "How much did this set you back?"

"Don't worry about that," Kekoa said. "We need to get it up and running by Friday."

"We reinforce everything, since this baby's gonna crank with the turbo," Sonny said. "You do the lube system, and I'll handle the exhaust. After that, we'll need to attach a new oil drain line to the turbocharger."

"Shouldn't we mount it first?" Kekoa asked. None of his friends back in Hilo had turbos—most just ramped up the horsepower with gimmicks—but this was the real thing.

"It's easier to do other work first. It's an expensive kit. You don't want to hurt our baby."

Kekoa nodded in agreement. It was his car,

but over time, it had become Sonny's car too. And now they had a silent partner.

Kekoa waited just outside the school grounds until the private security guard at the gate stepped away. Part of Kekoa wanted to smash the gate, but he knew better. He put the car in park, jumped out, opened the gate, and drove inside the grounds. With its long, winding entrance, the driveway of White Sands Prep would have made a perfect drift course, but that's not where he and Billy would race. There was only one place to compete: Tantalus.

Kekoa parked his car in front of the school entrance and looked at his phone. School was just about over, but it was well past time that somebody taught Billy Cain a lesson. Who better to beat someone who had everything than someone with nothing to lose?

CHAPTER EIGHTEEN

"What's he doing here, brah?" Billy asked Ryan when he saw Kekoa leaning against the Nissan. Ryan had apologized to Billy and was back in the group, for the time being.

"If Adila's with him, we'd better direct them to the servant's entrance," Shane said. Ryan laughed really loud, but Billy just stared ahead.

"What do you want?" Billy walked closer to Kekoa with Ryan and Shane close behind.

"Your car."

Billy laughed. "I don't blame you. But

I'm not giving it to you. My old man's big on charity, but not me."

Kekoa crossed his arms over his chest. "We'll race for it."

Billy scratched his head. "And if I win, I get that thing?"

"Sure, you don't need my ride," Kekoa said. "You could buy ten of them. But think about what it'd be like actually to earn something on your own."

"Look, brah, it's not happening."

"You got everything. Everything but guts, that is."

Shane and Ryan hooted. "Billy, man, don't let this hood punk talk to you like that."

"Like I said, it's not happening." Billy started to walk away, quickly.

Kekoa yelled at Billy. "Adila said you're almost eighteen but nowhere near a man."

Billy turned on his heel and laughed at Kekoa. "Nice try."

Ryan and Shane formed a wall as Kekoa walked toward Billy. "You've got a better car and you say you're a better driver, so I can't figure it out. What are you afraid of?"

Billy grew silent. He thought about Tucker, but when he looked at Ryan and Shane, he knew he had no choice. He could always back out if he couldn't figure out a sure way to win. "Okay."

CHAPTER NINETEEN

"Why are you doing this?" Adila asked for maybe the hundredth time.

Kekoa's nerves were as solid as the Nissan's chassis. "I can't explain it, but there's something about him . . . Especially that story about cutting the kid's hair."

"I know, somebody's got to put him in his place. But why you, Kekoa?" Adila asked, holding back tears.

They sat in Kekoa's ride. He'd installed the passenger's seat and taken Adila on some drifts through the projects. At first, she was scared, but he showed her that he knew what he was doing.

"If not me, then who?" Kekoa said. "Besides, what else have I done with my life? This is one thing I can do better than anybody my age. And I want to prove it."

"How are you going to do that?" Adila asked.

Kekoa reflected on how he had goaded Billy Cain into racing up and down Tantalus Mountain. They would go up together, and one would come down first. Kekoa knew he could win if Billy Cain played by the rules, but he doubted that Cain would. People like that thought they were entitled to their own set of rules. Kekoa would need to be fast. He'd also need to be cautious of whatever tricks Cain and his crew might try to pull.

CHAPTER TWENTY

Billy brought an army with him. Not just Shane and Ryan but all White Sands drifters. He recruited some navy brats and Japanese kids too. Billy knew he stood a better chance if others were involved. If need be, one of them could take out the hotshot *hapa*.

"I got so much power, I might fly to the moon," Billy said to Shane on the phone. They were all parked near the base of the mountain in the parking lot of Hanahau'oli School.

Shane laughed. "We got your back. You got nothing to worry about. Except . . ."

"Except what?" Billy asked.

"What about the cops?" Shane asked.

"Another reason to have all of you around." Billy would win not only because he had the better car but because he was smarter than everyone else. "If the cops show, they can't arrest all of us. So some Japanese kid gets cuffed. What do I care? I'll be out front, so they'll never catch up with me."

"That's a great idea because—"

"He's here." Billy hung up the phone and buried it in his pocket. He turned on the video camera mounted on the dash. He wanted every moment of his victory preserved on film.

"What's going on?" Kekoa shouted as he climbed out of his car. He walked toward Billy's Toyota. Billy bounded out of his car and met Kekoa halfway.

"Change of plans?" Kekoa said.

"Read the fine print, *hapa*." Kekoa stood mute as Billy dictated the rules by which he would race, which included all the other cars being involved. "Take it or leave it."

Kekoa shrugged. "Got nothing else to do tonight."

Billy looked past Kekoa and into his car. There was someone in the passenger's seat. "Is your Kenyan friend afraid to talk to me? She should get out and give me a good luck kiss."

Kekoa turned and waved. The Nissan door opened, and out stepped Keiichi Yamada.

CHAPTER TWENTY-ONE

"Thanks for the turbo," Kekoa said to Keiichi.

"Humiliate him in front of everyone. That's all the thanks I need," Keiichi said. They fist bumped, and then Keiichi was gone. Seconds later, Sonny appeared at the car door. He stuck out his hand.

"Kekoa, this is it. We sweated over this car. Now make it sweet. Beat this guy," Sonny said.

Kekoa shook his hand, hard.

"Save your strength for that clutch," Sonny added. He gave Adila the last word.

"Kekoa, tell me you're going to be safe,"

she said. "Tell me you're not going to get hurt."

"I'll tell you all of that when I'm the first one back here."

Adila kissed his cheek.

"Tonight, I prove my name," Kekoa said. "I am Kekoa. I am courage."

While the cool of the early evening rolled in from the ocean, Kekoa was distracted by the splendor of Hanahau'oli School. He recalled his school in Hilo: broken desks, shattered windows, and unpaved parking lots. His grandma probably made less money a year than it cost to send a child to Hanahau'oli for a semester. Billy Cain went to a school like that. Kekoa wouldn't only prove his name tonight but Adila's name too: justice.

Jack O'Brien stood between the two cars. Just like Kekoa had seen in hundreds of videos, Jack held his arms in the air, stared at both drivers, and then dropped his hands to mark the start of the race. Although Kekoa had installed the turbo, his car didn't have the nitrous boost that shot Billy into the first drift.

Kekoa followed behind, executing perfect drifts as he reached the hard left at Makiki Street onto Round Top Road. Kekoa realized instantly what Billy was doing. Billy wasn't just drifting because that was the smartest and quickest way to navigate hard turns; he was creating a smokescreen. The cloud of burnt rubber and exhaust smoke blinded Kekoa just as he needed to execute his drift. Billy had raced this mountain with others, Kekoa realized, while Kekoa had only drifted it alone.

The turbo roared as Kekoa pushed the Nissan up Round Top Road, the beginning of the mountain climb. In his head, he recalled the map of the mountain road and tried to figure out where he could overtake Billy. He couldn't pass Billy in a straightaway, so he'd need to wait until near the end—a series of hairpin turns where the best drifter would win.

Behind him, Kekoa heard other cars, but he had stripped the rearview mirror so he couldn't make out how many. At the first tricky turn, Kekoa kept control of his out-of-control car and seemed to gain on Billy, who had run off the road navigating a near U-turn before leaving the residential streets. As he drove past where Billy had run off the road, Kekoa saw a busted mailbox.

In the straightaway, Keiichi's turbo paid off. He closed on Billy. At the next massive U-turn, Billy drifted perfectly and kept his lead, but Kekoa knew he was gaining. Coming out of the drift, his feet danced heel-and-toe on the pedals, working together as quickly and efficiently as the pistons in the engine.

Kekoa sensed he was gaining but also sensed something growing near. The feeling grew inside him: a car was close, closing, and then *clang*!

The collision shoved Kekoa forward—his chest bounced off the steering wheel. He shook off the pain and floored it. Behind him, he heard the sound of the car going into a drift or maybe a spin. Then a crash. Kekoa raced on.

He had fallen behind because of the rear-ending. He only caught site of Billy as Billy began to drift through the road's winding way. A scenic lookout point signaled the halfway point, Kekoa guessed he was ten seconds behind. In life, that was nothing. In a race, it was everything.

As he crossed the merger with Telephone, Kekoa saw oncoming lights. He slowed down. Even though he had the right-of-way, you never knew about other drivers: who wouldn't be paying attention; who might be breaking the law, like him, Billy, and everybody else out on the mountaintop. Kekoa didn't hear the roar of other cars in the distance anymore, so he was far ahead of almost everybody else. But he was still in second.

Kekoa took a deep breath when he saw a series of S-shaped turns through the darkness. The speed limit said twenty miles an hour. He kept it at forty and punched it up to fifty on the few straightaways. Cold mountain air sucked into the intake system. Resentment burned in Kekoa's veins and pushed him to drive faster, drift harder.

Coming off the mountain, Kekoa saw Billy's car. It looked as if Billy had spun off near the mountain's last big turn. Just as Kekoa was about to blow past, Billy's red Toyota sprang like a waiting tiger. Kekoa pulled the e-brake, not for a cheap drift but to save his life. Surrounded by a cloud of smoke, both cars pushed toward the finish.

As Kekoa tried to focus on the race, his mind raced as well. Had Billy tried to crash into him? Kill him?

The final miles took Kekoa and Billy onto Makiki Heights Drive, into wealthy neighborhoods and past places like the Hawaii Nature Center, another place that no doubt ran on Cain money. They raced neck and neck down the two-lane road with Kekoa on the left, Billy on the right. After every mile, drift, turn, and twist, the race would come down to just a few seconds.

CHAPTER TWENTY-TWO

Billy sat in his car, head down, mouth open, and eyes closed. He'd never lost at anything before, so like a child taking its first step, he felt awkward. He snatched the camera from the dash and erased the video. He wanted to believe there'd be no proof, but he knew better. The proof was in the silence of his phone. Unlike every other race, where congratulations texts had flooded in, he was alone in defeat.

"You okay?" Billy heard someone yell as the guy tapped on the window glass. Billy wiped his eyes and then opened the window. Kekoa stood outside.

"Great race." Kekoa extended his hand. Billy kept his hands in his pockets.

"Pay up," the skinny white kid said. Kekoa's buddy must have followed after the other racers drove across the mountain.

Billy surveyed the inside of the Toyota that failed him. It was the car's fault, not his.

"Sonny, relax, give him a minute," Kekoa said.

Billy turned off the car, removed the key, and opened the door. He couldn't look at Kekoa, so he glanced past him to where his friends stood. Billy waved. No one waved back.

"Here." Billy tossed the key on the ground in front of Kekoa. "You won it, but so what? It's not the best drift car. If it was, I would've won, since I'm the best drifter on the island."

Kekoa laughed but didn't say anything. He also didn't bend down to get the key.

"What's so funny?" Billy asked as he walked away from his defective ride.

"You. You think you're special, but you're

not. You can buy everything: cars, friends, and other people's lives. But that doesn't make you special," Kekoa said.

Billy said nothing as he walked past Adila. She wasn't that pretty anyway. Besides, one of his father's friends had a maid from Africa. Maybe she had a daughter. He'd get with her instead. Billy opened his phone, punched a number, and called for a limo to pick him up.

CHAPTER TWENTY-THREE

"That is one ugly baby," Kekoa said, then laughed.

Sonny patted the hood of the Nissan. "Maybe, but it's my baby. I–I mean, we—built it up from scratch." Some of the empty part boxes still lay strewn about Kekoa's grandmother's garage.

Kekoa offered his grease-stained hand, and Sonny shook it.

Adila applauded. "You got any money left to pretty it up? Girls like a pretty car."

"And a pretty boy." Sonny jabbed Kekoa's

shoulder. "Too bad I spent my half."

"I still don't understand why you sold Cain's car instead of keeping it," Adila said. "There was nothing wrong with it."

"Except the smell of defeat and his stinky cologne," Sonny said.

"The thrill is building the car yourself or with help from friends," Kekoa said.

"And the other guy's enemies," Adila added.

Kekoa remembered that he owed Keiichi Yamada a call.

"You know anything about baseball?" Kekoa asked. Adila and Sonny nodded. "Guys like Billy Cain are born standing on third base and think they hit a triple. Guys like us, we get hit by a pitch to get to first, steal second, and make it to third on a fly out. We earned the base. That counts."

Adila smiled. "I saw him the other day in a blue Honda with Nabika, a girl from school."

"He still thinks he's king," Sonny laughed.

"There's only one king of the mountain," Kekoa said. "And you're looking at him."

"That's because we haven't raced yet!" Sonny replied.

Kekoa stood lost in thought. Even though he could drift, Kekoa knew his life still lacked direction. He didn't know come June if he'd stay on the island or go to live with his mom. As he looked at Sonny and Adila, he thought about his drift-car list. Maybe stripping everything away was the first step in making a drift car, but he knew now it was a bad life lesson. Other people didn't weigh you down. They lifted you up—all the way to the top of the mountain.

THE NISSAN SKYLINE

MODEL HISTORY

The Nissan Skyline has been in production in some form since 1957. The Nissan Motor Company of Japan has made Skyline sedans, coupes, and even station wagons over the years. But fans of performance cars and of racing know the

Skyline for its GT-series sports cars.

In 1964, the Skyline made Japanese racing history when it managed to lead a Porsche 904 for a lap at a famous race at Japan's Suzuka track. The Skyline didn't win, but it took second. All of Japan noticed that a Japanese car could compete with one of the most famous European brands in racing.

Beginning in the 1980s, the R30 series of Skylines won the hearts of car enthusiasts. With straight-six engines and turbochargers, the Skyline coupes won a loyal following among street racers and tuners in Japan.

The Skyline had a reputation beyond Japan. Nissan didn't sell these sporty Skylines in the United States for most of the model's life. But video games, movies, and magazines all helped to create a cult following for the car, and some were imported by enthusiasts.

SIGNATURE MOVES

Skyline sports cars have always been available as rear-wheel drive vehicles, and this makes them ideal for drifting. Skylines are legendary as drift racers.

What exactly is drifting? A driver can make a car slide or "drift" through a corner by oversteering—turning more sharply than necessary—at the beginning of a turn so much that the rear wheels lose traction. A skilled drifter can continue through the corner by turning the front wheels so that they're eventually heading in the opposite direction of the turn.

According to the website for Formula Drift, the organizers of a drift racing series, "In Japan, the art of Drifting has been popular among the street racers or 'hashiriya' for more than 15 years, and has morphed into one of the country's number one attended motorsports in less than a decade, where professional Japanese Drifters are the equivalent of national celebrities."

THE SKYLINE ON FILM

The Skyline's most famous appearance might be *2 Fast 2 Furious*, the second movie in *The Fast and the Furious* series. Brian O'Conner, played by actor Paul Walker, drives a heavily tuned Nissan Skyline GT-R (R34).

THE SKYLINE TODAY

Nissan continues to produce cars for the Japanese market under the Skyline name. Nissan introduced a very limited edition coupe in 2011 to commemorate the fifty-fifth anniversary of the Skyline in 2012.

KEKOA'S NISSAN SKYLINE

ENGINE: VQ35HR V6 engine, 2.5 liter, 225 horsepower (this was *before* the turbo kit was added); six-speed manual transmission; installed a cold air intake system, new fuel pump, and hoses; did an oil change and installed a new oil drain line; installed performance spark plugs and wires; replaced air filters (these remove the dust particles from the air before they go into the engine); and of course, upgraded horsepower with turbo kit (I've seen a big increase in power when I'm cruising uphill. It's also more efficient and quieter than it was before the install)

DRIVETRAIN: throttle body coolant; power steering system flush; installed a brand-new performance clutch kit (helps the car control all the horsepower it's producing)

SUSPENSION: installed stabilizer anti-roll bars (these help reduce the roll of the vehicle and keep the tires in contact with the road); installed a coil-over damper kit and new struts; tightened struts and springs; installed an LSD (limited slip differential)—these can be expensive, but they're essential when drifting, and they drive more horsepower toward the ground, making it easier to make sharp turns; power steering system flush; adjusted the camber using a camber gauge I found in grandpa's garage

BRAKES: installed new front and rear brake pads; upgraded to a performance rotor kit; brake fluid flush; replaced parking brake (the guy who owned it before me must've drifted, too)

WHEELS/TIRES: upgraded to performance tires—no rims for me (they add too much weight!); also planning on getting some performance wheels once I save up some more money

EXTERIOR: painted body with fresh coat of light blue; installed splash guards (for those nights when it's wet and muddy out there. They only add a couple pounds—I think it's worth it to keep my Nissan looking sweet)

INTERIOR: stripped out all the extra weight on the inside of the vehicle; needle calibration on gauge faces; new steering wheel; new shift knob

ELECTRONICS: upgraded to a new speaker system; installed flywheel; installed a new fuel injector

Check out the rest of the ***TURBOCHARGED*** *series:*

THE
CATCH
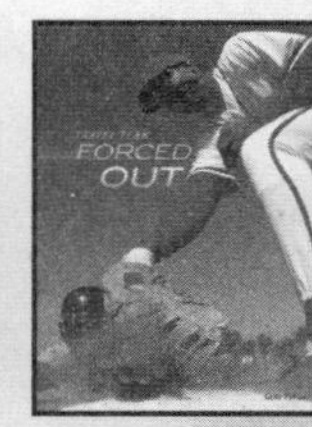
FORCED
OUT

HIGH
HEAT

OUT OF
CONTROL

POWER
HITTER

THE
PROSPECT